T0207802

The Dream App

The Dream App

FAHEEM NAJIY

THE DREAM APP

iUniverse books may be ordered through booksellers or by contacting:

iUniverse
1663 Liberty Drive
Bloomington, IN 47403
www.iuniverse.com
1-800-Authors (1-800-288-4677)

Because of the dynamic nature of the Internet, any web addresses or links contained in this book may have changed since publication and may no longer be valid. The views expressed in this work are solely those of the author and do not necessarily reflect the views of the publisher, and the publisher hereby disclaims any responsibility for them.

Any people depicted in stock imagery provided by Thinkstock are models, and such images are being used for illustrative purposes only. Certain stock imagery © Thinkstock.

ISBN: 978-1-5320-2436-8 (sc)
ISBN: 978-1-5320-2437-5 (e)

Library of Congress Control Number: 2017908210

Print information available on the last page.

iUniverse rev. date: 06/27/2017

This original work of fiction is constructed with soulful imagination and intrigue as it follows the daily exploits of three young female protagonists who grapple with a variety of contemporary themes in ways designed to arouse curiosity and incite an unbridled sense of wonder. The familiar drivers taxiing us through these adventures will be—well, you know what they say?

A familiar rhetorical question that opens doors and allows for the dissemination of timely tidbits of mundane and spiritual wisdom is derived from lengthy and diverse human experiences that prove they withstand the test of time. Call them axioms, adages, or just plain and simple insight into the unpredictable way life really works, even as we allow their anecdotal audacity to guide and protect us from narrow and hasty conclusions. Then we all should take solace in knowing these road maps were created by an intellect much greater than our own and are commissioned to be among us forever.

Like any story about life, the principle players in this tale are good and evil, and during these troubled times in the history of our species, where the so-called social media has given birth to a culture of antisocial behavior, our hope is for moral imperatives to compel readers to see themselves through the eyes of these young ladies and begin to think, feel, and learn while being entertained. And so it begins.

1

ALPHA

Gina awoke startled and gently soaked, as if she'd risen from a pool of water. Though groggy, she steadied herself on the bedside and recalled words from Grandpa Ricky, who'd told her when she was about three years old that there were times in all people's lives when they would need a stick man, a go-to person they depended on to say and do the right things during difficult times. The stick man's words and actions always helped people be the best of who and what they were.

So without hesitation, she wobbled slowly down the hallway, seeking the one person who could ensure she understood the message in last night's hauntingly vivid dream.

She called out to her in silence, "Nana?"

Gina was very close to her mother, Ginger, an administrative attorney for the mayor's office in Long Beach. Ginger was responsible for instructing Gina with a need to always display good manners and self-respect. She also taught Gina to think for herself and to never accept not knowing as an option. The hectic pace inside the mayor's office, along with Gina's extracurricular school activities, allowed only so much time for them to spend together each week.

Gina and Nana, on the other hand, were two sides of one soul who shared a world of mystery and imagination, leaving no subjects untouched during their many spirited and soul-stirring conversations that exposed Gina to Nana's unconventional views of the world. Those views would shape Gina's understanding of practically everything, with one of the earliest offerings being

"Everythang ain't for everybody, baby."

Gina was barely four years old.

"Some stuff you kin tell anybody, but other stuff you be careful about who you tell it to. Most folk kin only see thangs one way, but God gives some of us a different way to see life, so you got to be ready to act different 'cause of how you see thangs."

The closeness of their relationship was enough to prompt a curious four-year-old to inquire about the gender-specific nature of a stick man with Grandpa Ricky one morning. "Nana is the only one who is always there to answer all my questions and show me what to do, but she's a girl too, Grandpa Ricky. So can a girl be a stick man?"

Picking her up with his kind, massive hands and settling her gently on his knee, he offered his huge, hypnotic grin and said, "The *man* in stick man ain't like what me and your daddy are, baby girl. The man in the stick man means more like the man in the word *human being*, meanin' anybody that loves you enough to make sure you always okay. And yeah, baby girl, you ain't never gone know a better stick man than your grandma."

Though talking was Gina's and Nana's favorite form of communication, there were times in public when they shared knowing glances without spoken words, secretly speaking to each other's minds what other people shouldn't hear.

Gina had discovered this phenomenon while they shopped at a Ralph's Supermarket one day. She saw a young boy in line ahead of them with his pants sagging below his behind. He was wearing a T-shirt short enough to allow his underwear to be seen.

Nana gave her this look and said without speaking, *"That's the most disrespectful 'n' foolish thang these young boys ever took a hold to."*

Gina thought she was going bananas, so she quickly asked, "Nana, did you just say something to me?"

Again without opening her mouth, she told Gina, *"Baby, you heard me jest fine."*

Nana always asked for and showed genuine interest in Gina's opinions, telling her to be sincere when reaching a conclusion. She never tried to manipulate her perspectives and was always attentive. The influences from her mother's academic pragmatism, along with Nana's mundane/ethereal perspectives, helped Gina soar with the streamlined self-confidence of a high-flying peregrine falcon searching for its dinner.

At four toot ten and a slight 115 pounds of robust, unbridled energy, Nana also proved to be the favorite of Gina's best friends, Bobbi Li and Chrissy McFarland, who once told her in perfect harmony, "It's kinda spooky the way Nana knows what we're about to do before we even know it."

Prior to Gina's entering first grade, Nana and Grandpa Ricky had shown Gina thousands of photos of people she didn't know but hoped to someday. And her curiosity was placated with stories about country folk cousins who lived in rural Lafayette, Alabama. (Locals pronounced it as *La fett.*) Some folks said they possessed jackrabbit speed, could outrun cars, and occasionally had to run down slippery pigs desperately trying to avoid becoming a pork chop dinner at evening and fresh bacon for tomorrow's breakfast.

There were accounts of guinea hens laying eggs with shells hard as bricks and drawing water from a deep ground well so cold and fresh-tasting that it made tongues curl with joy. Lastly, there was the specter of a mysterious practice of some kinfolk who worked roots on people for good and bad results. All those photos and juicy stories had piqued Gina's interest in all things southern and made her grandparents runaway favorites in her heart.

"I've heard all those stories too, Boo Boo." Ginger was

consistently practical and sought to temper her daughter's love of those stories with regular doses of restraint. "But there is an old saying that you should only believe half of what you see and none of what you hear."

"You saying those things aren't true, Mama?"

"Ain't no way I'm sayin' such a thang, baby." Her tone was permeated with smiles, and she channeled her inner Nana. "Just want you to take account of what you're taught in school and add that to information gleaned from reading and research. Then use those things as tools to guide you to a better understanding of where the truth lies. Your grandparents are the Grios of our clan, honey. It's their mission to make sure each generation takes pride in what their predecessors did and what they knew, but it's only meant to buttress what your group learns and accepts as the truth in your own lives."

Gina's first vivid dream at age six was about her teddy bear, whom she called Teddy, and how he just disappeared one day. And no matter how hard she and others searched for him, Teddy couldn't be found anywhere.

She and Teddy were strolling through El Dorado Park, hand in hand on a crisp, sunshiny day, and the gentle breezes brushing against their cheeks were alive with energy and sweet jasmine. Stopping to take sips of warm water from a fountain and swelling their jaws full, they playfully chased and squirted water at each other, laughing hysterically. Then Gina and Teddy squatted under the canopy of a bushy oak tree to rest.

Since receiving him as a gift from Grandpa Ricky, she and Teddy were now inseparable, and Gina could never see herself without him, telling her mother one day, "When I go off to college, Mama, they better have a room big enough for both of us 'cause Teddy said I can't leave him behind."

This prompted a broad smile and this response from her mother, "Last I checked, Boo Boo, all the dorm rooms were more than big enough for young ladies carrying fuzzy little teddy bears."

So with Teddy snuggled up to her, they slipped into a nap, resting against the trunk of that gigantic oak tree. And when Gina awoke, her stomach was tied into knots because Teddy was gone. They searched everywhere throughout the day without finding Teddy. In the excitement, she never noticed Grandpa Ricky was not part of the search party.

For three days, it rained and rained and rained, keeping Gina inside, where she cried and cried and cried. On day four, the rain stopped, and she hurried outside and immediately found Teddy lying facedown in a small pool of water.

Picking him up, she asked, "Are you feeling all right?"

He didn't answer.

"Where have you been?"

Still he did not answer. He wasn't the same. Something was wrong with Teddy.

Everything in that dream seemed so close, so colorful, and so real, and it didn't frighten her. But it was confusing because, upon awakening, Teddy was beside her in bed, just like always. Knowing instinctively where to seek help with what it all meant, the six-year-old crawled out of bed with Teddy in tow and ran straight to Nana.

"What is it now, baby?" Nana saw the concern in her eyes and felt some of the same nervousness that was present when Gina was a six-year-old, though now she was trying to be reserved.

As she wrapped a warm blanket around the child's damp body, her reflection was on how there hadn't been any of those colorful dreams in over ten years and the eerie way that first one had foretold the death of the poor child's grandfather.

"The sight done come back again, huh, baby?" Nana already knew.

"Yes, ma'am." Very hesitant, the sixteen-year-old felt a need to speak more rational and mature about her concerns, not with the excited child speak of a six-year-old.

"I remember you said it could be a one-shot deal or maybe

become something that's just a part of me. Well, if this turns out to have meaning, it can't be ignored. I don't want to miss the message that it might be sending to me."

Had they considered there might be associative factors to her dreams ten years ago, maybe the end result could have been different. Because of the rapid onset of Alzheimer's disease, Grandpa Ricky became disoriented. He walked away from home one day and couldn't be found.

Four days after Gina's first dream, a sheriff's helicopter flying over the aqueducts channeling the Los Angeles River out to the ocean finally located him. He had drowned, found facedown in the slow-moving stream, just as Teddy had appeared in a pool of water in the dream.

After his funeral, which took place on a warm autumn day in Lafayette, Alabama, and would be the occasion that finally gave Gina a real taste of the South, Nana pulled her aside and tearfully said, "You come find me quick if any of them dreams come to you again, baby. That way we can kin ahead of thangs 'n' try to figure out what the Lord wants us to know."

The dreams were back now, and she was determined not to allow another person to suffer the same fate as her grandfather, who at six feet six and weighed two buttermilk biscuits shy of 290 pounds, was a great big bear of a man.

"I'll put the tea pot on while you gwown in the bathroom 'n' dry off some, baby. Then let's have a warm cup of tea 'n' milk while you tell me exactly what you saw. And don't you leave nothin' out, baby. Tell it all to me."

"I floated last night through a world of make-believe and wonder, totally cognizant that, up till now, there had been no experiences in my life to compare with this first-signs-of-spring freshness in the air, the luscious, richly vibrant colors adorning every tree, every batch of shrubbery, and anything identifiable as vegetation. No sky had ever been so hypnotically blue, and no sunshine was so stunning and so

warm. No other human beings were to be seen anywhere, just me and all the other life-forms abounding, abiding. Though the air was alight with the busy sounds of nature, I never knew there could be such quiet. I rested comfortably atop a plush, richly green lily pad, and it was the epitome of peace of mind. It felt Adam-like, how it must have felt to be the first person ever created and the parent to every successive generation. No bothers, no worries, no fears, as if everything around me sensed my presence and was alive with complete recognition of me.

"In front of me was a gigantic lake of deep blue, clear water that accepted the measure of sudden warm breezes sweeping across its face and depositing invigorating, rejuvenating, scant sprays of moisture gently wet upon my skin. It felt wonderfully divine. And who can resist when water beckons?

"Rising to my feet, I launched myself from my lily pad, springboarding into the awaiting coolness of life's most abundant component. Splash! The loving liquid cased me round like the warmth of my mother's womb, and I loved that feeling as I have never loved anything before. Emerging from the cooling waters and turning my face toward the bright, smiling sun, I closed my eyes and thanked the Creator of these magnificent surroundings.

"Just then, two small brown frogs went swimming by on the lake, and as they did so, they turned to me with looks on their ruddy frog faces that bade me to identify them. I quickly said, 'Lil dude and Cocoa, right?'

"One little frog's head tilted left; the other tilted right. And then gigantic smiles split their faces, confirming the accuracy of my identification as they turned and puffy little legs propelled them downstream. Feeling compelled to follow, I slowly swam after them, through the clearing and into an area where knotty tree branches of green, gold, and various shades of brown extended across the waters, like curtains of an opening act. Our swim continued until we reached a clearing of the riverbank, needing only a frog docking sign to have been more inviting.

"As I kept to the overhanging branches as they took to solid ground, *a strange foreboding shook me and prevented my turning about to leave. Something bade me to stay and continue my observation of these two members of the Anura species. And though I knew them by name, they were not my friends.*

"Lil Dude and Cocoa hopped to a nearby knotted branch that snaked its way from under the brush, briefly pausing like two soldiers on bivouac, taking a much-needed break while the air sacs on the sides of their bumpy heads expanded and contracted with measured breathing. There was a sudden movement from an area covered with leaves of various hues, and resting there was a worm or very tiny snake, maybe?

"Lil Dude's attention was locked onto the movements, and he crept closer to the source, even while Cocoa remained motionless. Now barely a nose hair away from the worm, Lil Dude's slimy tongue quickly snaked out to retrieve this easy lunch, an act aligning him with the uncertainty of fate.

"While watching the sticky tongue pull the small worm into his mouth, I recoiled as the full measure of the worm came into view from behind the thick, leafy brush. The wild, eerie eyes of an angry lizard gyrated independently as it stretched its mouth to twice the size of its large head and circled behind Lil Dude, who still held a lock on a small portion of the lizard's tail. The lizard then clamped those expanded jaws filled with razor-sharp teeth down on him with incredible force, and the intense pain visited upon the frog was reflected as misery in his eyes.

"Being neither friend nor foe is the theme that awaits us each day, and whether we hunger for it or hide from it out of ignorance and fear, everything in life must and will constantly change. For Lil Dude, change came rapidly as life went from a possibility of longevity to inevitable brevity in frog years. Meanwhile, Cocoa was a study in indifference as he made no move to help his companion, and there was no display of alarm or fear. He made absolutely no movement at all for long, arduous minutes while watching an act that surely signaled the end of his travel mate.

"And as the incensed and too-determined lizard, whose pulsing *body was only slightly bigger than his intended prey, continued his effort to devour the frog, whose lower half was now completely enveloped by the huge mouth of this not-so-big lizard, things weren't going well for either party.*

"It would have been mercy had the frog been set upon by a predator sporting more than just an unusually large head and mouth but also possessed the body mass to complete the task of making a meal of him. He rested occasionally to catch a much-needed breath but was unrelenting in trying to force the frog down his throat, not realizing that succeeding would only spell his demise as well. Poor Lil Dude, paralyzed by the circumstances, stared blankly with the tiny piece of lizard tail still dangling from his dying mouth and waited for the end.

"Humans resting atop the food chain is supported by our ability to have intelligent thoughts, a fact clearly highlighted in this encounter. Had the lizard been capable of such thought, he would have realized the futility of his task, that is, the frog's body was too big to be consumed by a predator barely larger than itself, and freeing himself from his intended meal was impossible. Like a billboard riding high atop a building on Sunset Boulevard announcing the latest cinematic productions, these words flashed through my mind, 'Never bite off more than you can chew.' The conclusion in this wonderful, Eden-like setting with this sad, little brown frog and a too-determined, not-so-big lizard with an appetite and mouth larger than his capacity to consume was that they both had done exactly that.

"Standing in the open, I considered whacking the voracious, not-so-big lizard with a stick and prying the sad, little frog from its mouth, but before I could move, Cocoa did. He turned toward me with a bone-chilling, defiant stare blaring at me, saying, 'Don't you dare! Things are as they should to be.' Then he casually hopped from the knotty tree branch onto the lake's edge and disappeared into the cool, crystalline waters.

"'Never bite off more than you can chew.' These words kept running round and round in my mind like vibrant children on a playground recess, even while I watched their meaning play out in a life-and-death *struggle right before my eyes. When I could view no more, I slipped back into the clear blue waters and swam back to the place where this adventure began, never once being able to lose my mind from the plights of the not-so-big-lizard and the little brown frog. Then it occurred to me that a larger predator was bound to come along and discover a tasty two-for-one meal."*

Looking very drained and swallowing the last of her tea to refresh, Gina said, "Well, that's it, Nana. That's every bit of it."

"A two-for-one meal, hmm?" Nana repeated with no hesitation. "This jest means that old rascal Satan gone try to undo two people with one stroke." Rubbing her chin in deep contemplation, she continued, "Baby, seems to me that the bitin'-off-more-'n'-you-kin-chew stuff gone be real important as you go 'bout figurin' this thang out."

"But, Nana, aren't you going to help me figure this out?" Gina asked, looking puzzled.

"I kin only guide you along, baby. The sight's been given to you, not me. That jest means those answers are up in that pretty lil head of yorn, 'n your heart gone help you connect all the dots." Then looking deep into Gina's eyes, she smiled warmly and said without opening her mouth, *"You jest trust in your heart, baby. Jest trust in your heart."*

2

WHAT NOW?

Teens attending high school could expect a harrowing experience waiting around each corner in this upside-down world filled with nonstop spills and thrills. Some days were good; others were bad. Some language was good and pleasant, but there was also a plethora of brash, insensitive, profane bluster spewing from the mouths of many who tried to appear more in charge, as if a potty mouth made them larger among their peers.

The excitement built from the first steps into hallways bustling with prissy, estrogen-overloaded, look-at-me girls with their Venus-like, perfect little bodies. The standing over everyone's head basketball stars or thick, no-neck football jocks and their Adonis-like bodies leaking testosterone from every pore. All was juxtaposed with those kids displaying near-Einsteinian prowess attributed to mathletes, band geeks, or computer nerds and the really weird group who just loved science. All was blended together with truckloads of frenetic, knucklehead energy generated by everyone else on board. And one now had the typical daily mosaic of an American high school.

Most kids seemed to enjoy this thrill ride, though just as many were disparaged by it. High school was a place wherein lay a promise of daily discovery and enlightenment, although students must remain vigilant against possible destruction by peers in this raucous, five-day-a-week, inescapable juggernaut. But they must also understand how proper negotiations of these hallways could make them stronger and wiser from week to week. Or maybe not. After all, some dopes were dopes for life, right?

The hallways of Long Beach Polytechnic High School were overloaded with the spirit of achievements and successes. It began with such standout alumni in sports, like perennial pro basketball legend Mack Calvin, who starred on several ABA and NBA teams during a lengthy career. There was Chase Utley, Major League Baseball's six-time all-star infielder, and recently deceased Tony Gwynn the Hall of Fame all-star. All the while, spotlights were reserved for Willie McGinest, three-time NFL Super Bowl champion. And still shout-outs were sent to DeSean Jackson, current all-pro wide receiver/return specialist for the Washington Redskins.

In the worlds of entertainment, Poly High was also recognized as the home for several of the pioneers of the West Coast rap sound: the late Nathaniel (Nate-Dogg) Hale, along with fellow Dogg pound mates, Warren (Warren G.) Griffin and Calvin (Snoop Dogg) Broadus. And blossoming in the underclass to these future musical powerhouses was another future film star, now an A-list actress, Cameron Diaz. And there were many, many others.

Even with this impressive roll call of accomplishments setting the pace, Gina, Chrissy Mac, and Bobbi Li proved themselves skillful at managing these pathways from week to week, so they not only survived but thrived. And to keep them focused on enjoying this experience, Ginger would constantly remind this trio that there were no guarantees in life, that they were bound only by what they accepted as truth and to learn, see, and do as much as they can while they were young. It was sound advice but wrong about one thing because this peer group did have one slightly sinister guarantee that was as immediate and unavoidable as acne.

"The tardy bell, Gina! Hurry or we'll be late for civics class!"

Rushing through the hallways of Long Beach Polytechnic High School, Bobbi Li and Gina hustled to outrace the first period bell.

Gina Marie Bryant, Christiana Diana McFarland, and Bobbi Sun Li, or 3PG, as their peers had tagged them since fourth grade at Burnett Elementary, were an inseparable, highly energetic, insanely gifted trio who acquitted themselves well in all fields of expertise.

The 3PG moniker began innocently enough when Martine Guerrero, a classmate since second grade, was so impressed by how effortlessly the girls were always among the top five in every subject covered in classes. They also proved to be aces in choir practices and above-average gymnasts. They slammed their exhibits at science fairs and even rocked the sales of Girl Scout cookies.

In a classroom setting when the girls were once again being honored for their excellence in reading and spelling competitions, Martine proudly proclaimed them to be "Persistently Powerful Performers." That sentiment soon became gender-specific and then evolved into the acronym 3PG, the girls who personified persistently powerful performances, which quickly took flight among the student body and teachers alike.

So the girls decided to roll with it and chose to model themselves after their favorite powerhouse trio from the Cartoon Network, the Powerpuff Girls, an impish trio of wide-eyed superheroines whose superpowers were accidently created in a laboratory by their surrogate father, a bungling professor named Utonium. And being inseparable was the key element to them always outwitting and thrashing the unending parade of bad guys led by the irascible Tojo Mojo.

While shopping at the Gardena Swap Meet one Saturday

afternoon, the girls bought some colorful cotton T-shirts embossed with the images of the little heroines on them and regularly wore them to school in fourth and fifth grades. Gina, a pink freak, wore Blossom's image, while the blue of Bubbles was a natural for Bobbi Li. And the green of tough girl Buttercup was spot-on for Chrissy, as green also symbolized the luck of the Irish.

The 3PG were so committed to being front-runners in all aspects of their academic and creative functions that they basically lived on the honor roll, earning award after award for performance, so much that, by the time they entered Poly High School, each had earned a half semester of college credits by opting for extra classes in middle school rather than the traditional kinds of fun during the summer breaks. Sort of superhero-like they felt, they used their strengths to emulate those little cartoon babes they adored so much. And just like those little darlings, their fierce allegiance to one another was undeniable.

Gina was lanky at five foot five with smooth cocoa-brown skin and a bush of crinkly black locks adorning her head. Chrissy's athletic five-foot-nine frame and wavy flaming-red Irish curls spoke of European royalty. Or there was the slight build of the diminutive Bobbi Li, who, at five foot even, was always eye to eye with Nana. She had a natural straightness to her shimmering, jet-black mane that wrapped gently around a fresh face the color of golden honey. Except for their looks, one could easily have thought them to be siblings. This powerhouse trio was what the UN was intended to be, multicultured and the stronger because of it.

Chrissy and Gina had started first grade together, while Bobbi Li appeared like a guiding light in their second-grade classroom. And from that moment, they would spend nearly every waking hour at each other's homes, with sleepovers being so regular that it seemed each household had three daughters. Whether it was during outings at summer camps, on the swim teams, or the many field trips provided by the school, their synergy created a natural perceptibility among them that exposed troubling glitches in either of their behaviors, so they formulated an unwritten rule to confront all problems immediately.

Today appeared to be one of those times, so after observing Gina the entire duration of their lunch period, Bobbi and Chrissy could remain quiet no longer.

"Okay, what gives, Boo Boo?" Bobbi began with the pet name used only by Gina's closest family. "You've been like spacing this whole period, sister."

"Yeah, girl. What's really going through that thoroughly analytical brain of yours?" Chrissy teased. Then she turned serious and added, "This isn't anything about your dad, is it?"

Gina's father, Master Sergeant Maurice Bryant, was doing his second tour of duty in Afghanistan as an advisor, and they all constantly worried about him.

"Huh?" Coming back in focus, Gina responded, "No, no, sorry, you guys. I know I've been a little off center today, but no, Daddy's fine. Nothing new since the Skype I had with him two days ago, and you guys already know about that."

"Then what's up, girl? You starting to make us worry about you," Bobbi Li persisted.

"BFFs aren't supposed to be worrying about each other without knowing why," Chrissy added.

"Okay, okay, you guys. I was going to say something to you about this later. It's just got me a little worried right now, but I know you guys can probably help me figure this thing out," said Gina.

"Probably?" Chrissy feigned incredulous. "You hear Miss Thing, Bobbi Li?" Leaning over to face Gina almost nose to nose, she said, "When have we ever not helped you work through whatever comes up between us?"

"Chill, Chrissy Mac. You know she didn't mean it like that," Bobbi Li defended Gina.

"Well, that's the way it sounded to me," she said, stubbornly put.

"Pump the brakes, Chrissy, all right? So I misspoke. Don't

make it into a felony," Gina said, well-spoken by the daughter of an administrative attorney. "Sorry for not saying anything, but I've really been trying to figure out just what might be happening, okay?"

"That's why you have friends, member?" Chrissy's tone was needling.

"Oh-kay, Chrissy." Gina was now clearly annoyed.

"And your apology is accepted, Boo Boo." Chrissy's sarcasm hinted toward meaning a mistake and not the genial intent of Gina's nickname.

Rolling her eyes, Gina responded in kind, "I love you too, Chrissy Mac. And I'll see you guys at the house later, okay?"

As they walked down the hallway away from Gina and toward the science class they shared, Bobbi Li quickly admonished Chrissy, "That Irish temper of yours is way too much sometimes, you know? There was really no reason to press her like that, especially after she said she was sorry."

"Ahhh, leave me alone, Bobbi Li." Rolling her eyes, Chrissy was annoyed.

"Oh, you did not just say that, Chrissy Mac. And on what planet is that ever going to happen?"

When they arrived at the Bryant household around six and after greeting Gina, Chrissy and Bobbi Li took their obligatory face time with Nana. As their resident oracle, Nana always had information to absorb from each of them and, in turn, dispensed tidbits of wisdom streamlined to fit the person to which it was given, like the final admonition to Chrissy as she left the room that evening.

"Red, don't you leave that room tonight without lettin' them others know what's goin' on with you, you understand me?"

"Yes, ma'am, Nana. I'll make sure they know."

And this was what made Nana *Nana*. For her to know Chrissy had something that needed to be shared with Bobbi Li and Gina without it having come up as a topic in their one-on-one conversation was spooky.

3

EARLY LIGHTS

In Mrs. Alvarez's fourth-grade class, the 3PG's excellence in reading and word comprehension was off the charts as they once again led the way. The only other student touting that level of word comprehension and mastery of text was Yvonne Loomis, a taller-than-most, thick, young girl with smooth skin the color of a plain Hershey's chocolate bar and sad, brown eyes. She had an electric smile she seldom used. She seemed shy and quiet, never offering up her hands to answer questions during class although her test results confirmed she knew them easily. Hardly any of her fellow students engaged her socially, almost as if the combination of her being physically imposing and cerebral was more than they could handle, thereby relegating her to a lot of isolated moments during the course of the day.

That was until Gina Bryant stepped to her table at lunch one day and said, "Hello, tall person." The warm smile preceding her greeting disarmed Yvonne completely. "Mind if I sit with you today?"

"Sure your friends won't mind you sitting with the giant nerd of the class?" Yvonne tilted her head at an angle toward the table where Bobbi Li and Chrissy were seated.

And without her eyes moving away from Yvonne as she sat, Gina said, "They'll be fine, girl, but what I want to know is how you keep making the highest grades in science class? Please tell a sister you be busting your brains out studying, right?"

"Sorry, Gina, wish I could tell you I do, but I don't." Yvonne smiled briskly.

"Gee, thanks," Gina said, grinning. Yvonne matched her smile. "That really gets the old confidence krunk."

They laughed, and this would be the first time of many that Yvonne's classmates got to see that electric smile open up a normally stoic face, which was actually quite cute. This was what made Gina *Gina*. She always had the right words at the right times for the right person.

Bobbi Li and Chrissy had long accepted that Gina was unique, like a mini version of Nana, capable of clearly seeing some things not really understood by others. So when she earlier begged out of their regular lunch in deference to sitting with Yvonne Loomis, they already knew she was onto something they had yet to realize. She didn't leave them in suspense long.

"It was just a hunch, guys," Gina began as they walked up Lime Street toward Chrissy's house. "I wasn't really sure, but it seems I was right."

"About what, Boo Boo?" Bobbi Li questioned. "And there's no way we expected her to open up to you so easily."

"Yeah," Chrissy's tone was mocking, "What link did that Yeti, Yvonne open up to set your brain on a Google search, that she's the love child of Niagara Falls and Mount Vesuvius, maybe?"

"Chrissy, that was so unnecessary!" Gina scolded. "Out of all the things we love most about you, that acid tongue and snottiness when you don't understand something is annoying. And that's the problem here. It was a feeling like sticky syrup poured into my hand." She rubbed her index finger slowly against her thumb. "But I was right about what I felt, Chrissy. This girl really just does not like you."

"OMG! How will I ever survive that revelation?" She grabbed two handfuls of her fiery locks in a mocking gesture, but she knew from unsmiling faces they wouldn't let her pass this off as joke time.

"C'mon, guys. This is not the first kid we've known that just didn't like one of us, right?" Chrissy said, pleading.

"No, Chrissy." Gina was in her face now. "She really doesn't like you, as in willing to have a physical confrontation kind of way."

"Yeah, and she's probably the first girl that's big enough and tough enough to try to do something about it, Christiana Diana McFarland."

Using their entire names was always Bobbi Li's signal to them that they had brought her to the edge where she became a no-nonsense negotiator committed to resolving matters quickly and backing away from that edge, as one of her favorite human rights vanguards, Malcolm X, famously coined, "By any means necessary."

"So what I'm saying to you is," Bobbi Li continued, "from now on, you be the big girl and avoid any confrontations with Yvonne, understand?"

Gina took a defiant stance next to Bobbi Li, signaling to Chrissy she backed up every word.

And to quell any hint of rebellion, as was evident by the quizzical look on Chrissy's face, Bobbi Li gestured with her index fingers while repeating slowly, "Do you understand me, Christiana Diana McFarland?"

Chrissy was a very pretty girl with emerald green eyes and small, barely noticeable freckles atop her firm cheeks. She was also the acknowledged tomboy of the trio. She could outrun, outjump, outthrow, or outswim practically all her peers, except for Bobbi Li, who transformed into Olympic gold medalist Katie Ladecky in a pool of water. And for a girl who didn't particularly seem athletic, Gina could ball circles around Chrissy on the basketball court, having the game that assimilated the handles of WNBA champion Diana Taurasi and the lethal scoring prowess of WNBA champion Maya Moore. But otherwise, Chrissy could outwrestle and, in some cases, even outbox most boys at that age because of rigorous training provided by her two favorite uncles who promised they would see her in the Olympic Games one day doin' somethin', so they said.

Donny McFarland was once a world-class athlete who had been a running back at San Diego State. He had played triple-A ball in the LA Dodgers organization and spent six years as an NFL running back with the Seattle Seahawks from 1995 through the 2001 season. Her other uncle Sean had ruled the ring as WBA, WBC, and IBF lightweight champion of the world for six years, beginning in January 1993 and officially retiring in August 1999 with a final record of thirty-eight wins and only three losses. And he was a stickler for making sure ring announcers, Michael Buffer and Jimmy Lennon Jr., always pronounced his name Mick Farland and never Mack Farland.

Because of those two, there wasn't a boy or girl who would dare try Chrissy in any physical encounter. The boys mainly wanted to avoid the shame of going through life being that guy who had to bring his A game just to best a girl. The girls? Well, it was fairly obvious why they didn't want to try her. But that was prior to Yvonne Loomis's hasty transfer over to Burnett Elementary from Lakewood Elementary, prompted by her response to problems with a school bully whom she had lifted off his feet, held upside-down, and shook violently until he bawled like a baby and peed his pants. There was a slight foreboding permeating the student body and teaching staff afterward, which fed into parental complaints and numerous he-said-she-said issues, which finally led Yvonne's parents to move back to Long Beach and into the family home on East Twentieth Street.

So there wasn't going to be any confrontation between Chrissy and Yvonne that day or maybe never because of their intervention and firm admonishment. The 3PG was a tight-knit trio with respect and love for one another, and thank God, they also listened to each other.

4

THE ORIGINAL STICK MAN

Stick Man was one of those southern standards that became a metaphor for so many elements of Gina's life, just as most of those old stories had become. And although Grandpa Ricky provided her with the meaning of the term years earlier, it wasn't until after his death that Nana revealed its origin.

Hair-doin' time was the best for storytelling, and Gina would always sit cross-legged between Nana's legs while getting her thick, bushy hair either braided or twisted and moistened into locks. She concentrated on the tenor of each word as the diverse tones Nana baked into each juicy, thought-provoking story had a deep effect on her emotions.

"When Ricky was a boy, his family sharecropped on land owned by the Johnson family. Mike, Mr. Johnson's son, clung to Ricky tight'ern the belt he wore around his own little, narrow waist. And though black and white folks weren't supposed to back then, Mike told his folks and everybody else that Ricky was his best friend in life and always would be.

Nana said, "Me 'n' Ricky met when I was eleven 'n' he was fifteen. He wasn't studin' 'bout no little ol nappy head girl like me, but I knowed he was gone be my husband one day." She flashed a moon-sized grin. "Nobody spent mo time with him than Mike, though. They were inseparable. Come before they finished high school, they took n left for Chicago. And Ricky told me they took they little money earned from pickin' cotton 'n' bought some brand-new pool sticks 'cause only thang they loved more 'n' each other was shootin' pool. Then they set out to get rich. They made mo money playin' white men 'cause most of the blacks fellas they run into ain't had no mo money than they did.

"So they decided Mike would do the playin' 'n' Ricky would keep him focused 'n' make sure he stayed on top his game. He'd watch his back n tell him what stick to use on every shot, like whether to use a top spin or a bottom spin or a left or right side cut, that kinda stuff. And they spent four years runnin' all over everywhere, makin' plenty money, so they started sendin' some home to they mamas. Ricky creeped back home alone when I was 'bout a Halloween short of fifteen years old and never said a whole lot to nobody, but those of us seen him without Mike already knew somethin' was bad wrong. He looked real sad, like a man with part of his self missing. Found out later Mike was in jail for killin' a man in St. Louis, Missouri, after they done won more than twelve thousand dollars off him shootin' pool. The man stuck his finger in Mike's face and said he didn't think he needed to pay no ragtag Bama Cracker 'n' his colored boy sidekick. Then he stood defiant with six other men backin' him up. And two of 'em was holdin' guns in they hands. He say, 'Hey, boy, you gone and pick up this white trash and shuffle y'all's ass on back down South before I really get mad and decide that maybe y'all won't be missed if you don't show up no more.'

"That man was thumpin' his finger on your grandpa's chest. And Ricky said it felt like his angry heart was 'bout to jump out and grab 'em. Ricky say he could see in Mike's eyes how thangs was gone end up in a real bad way that night, especially after the ornery way that fella turned back at Mike 'n' said he expect him to leave a twelve thousand-dollar toll fee on top of that pool table.

"Mike was half Ricky's size but was ten times meaner, so before that fella took another breath, Mike slit his throat with a pocketknife, 'n Mike 'n Ricky made a bloody mess outta all them men that night. The worst thang happened was two of them men died at the hospital 'n' two others was fitted to wheelchairs for the rest of they lives afterward."

That recall brought moist sadness to Nana's eyes as she continued, "They took they money off of 'em but run into a roadblock tryin' to git outta that area. And Mike told Ricky to get out, take the money, and run through the woods while he led the police in the other direction. Ricky said no, that he wasn't gone leave his brother on his own. Then Mike remind him that these folk gone put him in jail, but he seen pictures of horrible thangs a mob would do to black folk. And he jest couldn't stand knowin' they done awful thangs like that to Ricky. He told Ricky, 'Listen, I'm yo stick man now, Ricky, so git yo butt on out this car 'n' run like hell, man!'

"He went to Mike's folks no soon'ern he limped back into Lafette to apologize to 'em 'bout what happened 'n' to give 'em Mike's part of the money. Mr. Johnson told 'im he didn't need to apologize 'cause they knowed him 'n' Mike loved each other like they was blood kin. Said Mike was always callin' home braggin' 'bout how him and his stick man was cleanin' up on the local pool playin' circuits. Said Mike done sent plenty money home so they wasn't gone have no problem lookin' after him in jail.

"He told Ricky to git far way from Alabama as soon as he could 'n' don't go tryin' to write or see 'bout Mike 'cause that be the easiest way for the police to find him. Ricky run way out to California, but three years later, he sneaked back into Lafette to see 'bout his mama 'cause she was kinda ill then. And I was visitin' 'n' lookin' after her that day like I normally did, still always askin' her 'bout Ricky.

"Then somethin' happened when he come through that front door. And we jest stared at each other after so long a time apart. It was like we both knowed he wasn't supposed to go back to California alone. Right at ten years later, we was livin' offa PCH and Santa Fe on the west side of Long Beach.

"And I was right fat with your mama inside me the day Ricky come to me cryin' like a baby. Me being pregnant was the best thang in his life, he said, but word come back from Lafette that them folks up in Missouri done sent Mike to the electric chair. Your grandpa's heart was broke all to pieces. Ricky had done lost his stick man forever, baby."

Nana's emotional recount ended with a deep, sorrowful sigh, and Gina could feel her anguish and pain in the quaking of her small body. Laying her head in Nana's lap, she wiped at the soft stream of sadness caressing her own face, a sad reminder they were both missing their great big teddy bear.

5

TEDDY BEARS DON'T DIE; THEY MULTIPLY

"This is how God turns one of your worst times in life into one of your best times," Ginger said, seeking solace from within for Gina, who had said she felt kind of bad because of how being in the South for for the first time in life brought her so much joy, but it was her grandfather's death that had brought her there.

As they walked barefoot and hand in hand through the lush green grass of the cemetery, this would be one of the few defining moments in Gina's life not directly prompted by Nana, but by the woman who inspired her most to seek excellence from within.

"Remember how I told you why we started calling you Boo Boo?" asked Ginger.

"Yes, ma am." Smiles alighted Gina's face. "You said Grandpa Ricky loved to joke and would sneak up behind you and Nana all the time with his big hands raised up like claws and shout 'Boo!' And then he'd laugh so hard at the way he scared you and Nana and how upset y'all would be because, no matter how many times he did it, y'all could never get ready for it."

"You do listen well, don't you, sweetie?" said an impressed mom.

"You said watching Grandpa Ricky laugh so hard was my favorite thing to see, so I would hold my hands up like claws and follow him through the house and out into the yard, hollering 'Boo!' Then me and Grandpa Ricky would be having crazy fun while I ran around, trying to scare everybody. But I don't really remember any of that, Mama." Gina's tears traced the innocence of her face and contrasted with a smile of pure joy.

Wrapping her daughter in loving arms, Ginger sought to simplify the complexity, "See how that darn old man still makes us smile and laugh, honey? And do you understand how bringing you here for this moment was his way of making all those stories and pictures come alive for you?"

"Oh, Mama, you just don't know." Retaking her mother's hand, excited, she was now leading the way through the grass while saying, "All my cousins, uncles, and aunts, they're mostly nuts, you know? But they're the greatest! Cousin Charmaine took me over to the Tuskegee University campus, and on the way there, she was playing old-school classics by somebody called the Commodores. And we rode along singing, "She's a brick---house,,,she's mighty, mighty, just letting it all hang out."

Smiles burst into laughter as she continued, "She said y'all used to do a dance called the bump on that song all night long when y'all were in college, Mama. She also said that all the Commodores attended Tuskegee and they started the band right there on campus. Then she showed me pictures of the Tuskegee Airmen who helped us win World War Two by being so badass. Oops?" Flustered, she apologized, "Sorry, Mama, but that's what she said."

"No matter, baby." Her mother smiled briskly. "Go on and finish your story."

"Well, while they were flying their planes, no harm came to any of the white pilots they had to protect. She said they couldn't even drink out of the same water fountains as those white pilots when they came back from the war." She searched her mother's face curiously, as if wondering whether she knew all these things before continuing. "And, Mama, it just felt like I was at home there, like there were all these classes and teachers just waiting for me and Teddy to show up."

"Oh, thank you so much, Daddy," Ginger was offering silent praise. *"And thank you, Lord, for my baby's happiness today."*

"And then, Mama, cousin Alayna took me over to where she goes to school at Auburn University. And I learned about 'Go Tigers' and 'War Eagles!' But when cousin Sylvester took me over to Tuscaloosa to the University of Alabama where he plays football, everybody over there hollers 'Roll Tide!' He said to forget about 'Go Tigers' and 'War Eagles.' And cousin Alayna told me to forget about 'Roll Tide.' They say, as part of this family, I have to choose one or the other, and I said I'm only seven and live in California and don't know about that stuff. Then they both said that didn't matter, and as long as I'm in Alabama, I had to choose one or the other because God don't allow nobody down here to straddle the fence. Mama, our family is crrraaazy!"

Ginger's continuous silent praises brought a stream of joy tracing down her flushed cheeks, *"Thank you again, Daddy, for bringing your granddaughter home, and thank you so much, Lord, for my baby's happiness this day."*

6

THE TALK

"We know that what Nana tells us is tailored specifically for who she's talking to." But Gina opened up with urgency, "There are things we have to put on the table for discussion right now."

The 3PG were an anomaly among millennials and generation Xers because they actually preferred talking to one another face-to-face as opposed to texts, Facebook, Twitter, Instagram, Snapchat, or any other electronic form of communicating. As kids, they learned that talking into the face of a real person in real time tended to increase the level of veracity between the speaking parties. And besides, they really loved talking to one another.

"Here's what's been bothering me, guys."

And Gina went on to elaborate on everything, the highly sensitized perceptions she got when other people were troubled, the unusual mental conversations between her and Nana, and finally her dreams—when they began, what the initial dream foretold, and what the entirety of the newest offering was.

And when she finished, Bobbi Li and Chrissy just looked at each other, mouths agape and speechless, creating a pregnant pause that lasted so long it became necessary for Dr. Gina Bryant to induce labor.

"Ladies?!" Gina snapped her fingers repeatedly. "C'mon now. I know this is a lot to swallow in one spoonful, but this is what you asked me about earlier, and time is of essence here."

There was more silence.

Then Bobbi Li began slowly, "Forgive me, Boo Boo, but my circuits are like overloaded right now."

"Yeah, Boo Boo," Chrissy finally animated. "Jeez! I need a minute to reboot, sleep on this stuff, and get back at you later."

"Goes for me too, girl," Bobbi Li added. "It's gotten late anyway, almost nine-thirty, and we do have school, so let's wrap this up and start again tomorrow, okay?"

"Sounds like a plan," Gina conceded.

Then Chrissy said, "Uh, guys, Nana would kill me if I didn't tell you this little bit of news." She responded to quizzical looks by saying, "Oh, it's nothing like Gina's revelation, but it's something I should've told you already."

The next fifteen minutes or so were filled with information about how Chrissy's and Yvonne's hiatus from hostilities had come to a halt because of a misunderstanding about a creepy guy, Dominique, the starting point guard on the basketball team and a boy Chrissy totally didn't like. He became the center of the recent friction between them because of Yvonne's budding relationship with him and a fast-spreading rumor about his interest in Chrissy as well. She said they sat down in the locker room, and she expressed no interest in the creepy guy. And for a day or two, it appeared to be behind them.

Fast-forward and they were once again in the locker room, preparing for volleyball practice. And as Chrissy sat her book bag inside the locker, a ring belonging to someone from the boy's championship basketball team fell out and onto the floor with a very loud ding!

"Everybody freezes. All eyes are on me as I pick it up for examination, and the first question out of my mouth was if any of them had any clue how it got there. And of course no one did.

I turn it in to the coach's office. And as far as I'm concerned, it's not worth pursuing, knowing I'd find out from Coach who it belongs to. Then I planned to step to whoever it was from there."

"Chrissy, please tell us that wasn't Dominique's ring?" Gina slightly shook her head in disbelief.

"Of course it was. I mean, how else could this ridiculousness play out?" Chrissy seemed very frustrated. "I don't know who planted that ring, but the moment I realized Yvonne was eyeballing me very suspiciously, I just knew something was up.

"Yvonne approached Dominique the next day, who naturally wasn't wearing his ring. And she asked him why, and you know that clown told her he must have misplaced it somewhere. A couple days later, Coach confirms it's Dominique's ring and believe me, if I ever find out who put that stupid thing in my locker, I am so going to pound the crap out of them!"

"OMG! Chrissy, please don't say another word unless it's good night, okay? Let's go get in the love bug [Chrissy's Volkswagen Beetle], and you get me home before I start spazzin' for real."

Bobbi Li was obviously drained and anxious, which hastened their hugs, their good nights, and their exits.

She and Chrissy remained unnaturally quiet on their way home, inwardly realizing the 3PG was now having their very first big girl crisis. Both deeply pondered on all that had been revealed tonight. Bobbi Li didn't raise an eyebrow at the fact that, instead of taking the quicker shot from the Bryant's home in North Long Beach which would have sent them south on Atlantic Avenue to take a left onto Ocean Boulevard, which ran straight into Belmont Shore, where the Li family resided, Chrissy drove the loop along the Pike and Queen Mary routes before finally heading back east to Belmont Shore.

Then after dropping off Bobbi Li, she headed toward home in the Los Coyotes diagonal, driving as slow as a weed head feeling a major buzz from what Snoop Dogg called that "sticky-icky-icky."

The serious concerns about their first burgeoning big girl crisis did not escape the third member of this trio either as Gina said her prayers mindfully this night before crawling wearily into bed.

7

CRISIS CENTRAL

Lunch period moped along, mired in the continuance of last night's silence. And as the jackrabbit, the large, colorful image of Poly High school's mascot and symbol of pride, eyed them with indifference from its position in the center of the cafeteria wall, Gina gazed upon her two companions curiously as they both gave a slight side-to-side shake of their heads, indicating it was not yet time to talk.

Mercifully, the bell sounded, and before they parted ways, Bobbi Li said, "My house tonight. Six o'clock start, okay? Chrissy, pick up Boo Boo, and I'll see you guys there." And without waiting for affirmation, she melted into the crowd faster than ever before.

Both Chrissy and Yvonne were recognized as volleyball prodigies. Both were naturals as middle blocker and equally adroit at serving up wicked drop shots that baffled opponents, with Chrissy serving as a southpaw and Yvonne as a righty. They were easily promoted to the varsity team before the end of their freshman year at Poly High. Consequently, they were invited to participate with the AAU squads as sophomores and juniors and were now being groomed to be members of the next US Olympic team.

Bobbi and Gina already knew this, but they didn't know until that night that Chrissy and Yvonne had just yesterday received letters of acceptance and welcoming to Stanford University (Chrissy) and UCLA (Yvonne) respectively, and that was for both academic and athletic merits.

"You jumped all over Boo Boo for not being forthcoming, and you sat there full of information that could've made matters a whole lot clearer. And you couldn't just blurt it out like you always do, huh? You give us that craziness about you and Yvonne and just left us dangling in the wind?" Bobbi was steamed with Chrissy.

But Chrissy fired back, "Weren't you the one who told me to shut up last night?"

"Yeah, you're right. She did say that," Gina said. "But nothing has ever stopped you from running your mouth before, Chrissy, so don't go using that as an excuse."

"Okay, okay, but for real, guys." Chrissy was contrite as she spoke. "You're right, and I've been dead wrong acting like a complete jerk. Boo Boo, my bad for leaning into you so hard when my own mix is totally nuts. I owed it to you to be more understanding when you tried to explain at school, especially with all that I've got going on."

The give-and-take; the willingness to accept scolding and correction and then show contrition; and the ability to cry, swear, laugh, and joke and then grow their understanding 360 degrees, always ending where they began in complete love and harmony, if not always in agreement, were the greatest strengths of the 3PG. Their consensus was that Chrissy and Yvonne's troubles were probably the subject of Gina's latest dream, but that also left several unanswered questions as to why Dominique seemed so committed to having them bump heads. And how could he have stashed that ring in Chrissy's locker? And if he didn't do it, who did?

They knew these questions needed answering before they could prevent any further confusion or damage, so Gina took the steering wheel by saying, "Bobbi, you go have a talk with Dominique and see if you can find out what this guy is really up to, okay? I'm going to put out my feelers and find out who put that ring in that locker. And, Chrissy, you do all you can to just be cool, girl, and give us a chance to handle this thing for you, okay?"

A curious nonresponsiveness in Chrissy's eyes provoked Bobbi Li to ask, "Chrissy, you wouldn't be considering anything other than finding an intelligent way out of this foolishness, right?"

There was no answer.

"Chrissy?!" There was urgency from Gina as well. "You are not going to blow a spot on the Olympic team or a chance to become a Stanford Cardinal, are you?"

There was still no answer. And for Bobbi and Gina, this behavior was unnerving on so many levels. Chrissy occasionally displayed an initial stubbornness and unwillingness to cooperate, but she eventually found a way to accept majority rule in their tight circle of democracy. And that wasn't happening now.

Bobbi Li's alarm grew. "Chrissy, what the heck is really going on with you, girl?"

Gina's intensity matched Bobbi's. "C'mon, Chrissy. Nobody's going anywhere until we know how deep this dumb stuff really goes."

Staring afar, Chrissy admitted, "She called me out, man. Said after practice Saturday she was going to holler at me about what's been a long time coming. I'm a McFarland, and there are no cowards in my clan. And I'm not about to be the first. I will see her after practice Saturday. I won't start anything, but I won't run from it either. I realize there's a lot to lose, but this is about my basic right to defend myself, and you guys know I do that very well. So if that girl puts her hands on me, it's a wrap. I may wind up starting college on the JC level and have to forget about making the Olympic team altogether, because I'm going to hurt that girl really, really bad."

Gina held her finger up to her lips to shush Bobbi Li from

saying whatever was about to leap from her mouth. Then she said smoothly, "Okay, Irish Whiskey, time for you to get me and you home."

Bobbi Li remained silent, sensing Gina had already formulated a next move and would seek her input soon enough. She hugged them good night and then sat at her computer desk and waited. By calculating the minutes it would take for Chrissy to get Gina home, she figured it shouldn't be long to wait for it.

"I wanna run to you ooh-ooh-ooh-ooh!"

Picking up her phone, Bobbi Li smiled at the sweet melody of the Whitney Houston ringtone.

"Gina, we got a real problem here, girl. Your entire dream is about to blow up right in our faces!"

"Oh, man. Bobbi Li, they're both ready to bite off way more than they can chew, and if we don't stop this, it will definitely become a two-for-one meal! You saw that vacuous look in her eyes, right? And resigning herself to losing a full scholarship is just too scary. But I'm so afraid for Yvonne too. No matter how tough she may be, we know Chrissy will serve her up something she can't digest. And that's going to cost them both big time! We got work to do in a real hurry, Bobbi Li!"

Bobbi Li said, "Then hurry-up girls we be, Boo Boo!" Then she added, "Uh, Boo Boo, I just gotta know, girl. Do you think the dreams might be like an app or something? Like maybe you could activate or control them by manipulating something in your head like a download?"

"The real answer is that I don't know yet, Bobbi Li, but if this is going to be a part of me forever, I really need to figure it out."

It was now Friday morning, the end of the school week but the beginning of a mad scramble to save their sister from herself. One might ask, "Why not simply solicit some adult intervention in this matter?" And the answer would be found in the natural state of human growth and development as teens feel they exist largely in a world inaccessible to adult understanding. They were too old to be marshaled around like small children, but their youth didn't allow a clear understanding of the consequences riding shotgun with every bad decision.

Lack of experience was to blame for this, and experiences can only be acquired over time, which they hadn't had a whole lot of. Also to enlist the aid of parents or other authority figures would only make them pariahs, lepers, or anathema to anyone under age eighteen and signal to their peers they were not ready for prime time.

West Side Story and *The Outsiders* were two iconic offerings from American cinema highlighting this phenomenon on film. These battles must be fought one way or another, either physically or intellectually, and consensus must be achieved among this peer group, even if by way of tragic circumstances, in order for true learning to take place. As Cocoa said, that dreamy, little brown frog from Gina's dream whose words provided the impetus for the 3PG's present unsettling dilemma, "Things are as they should be."

Having already formulated their plans of attack by way of a very early morning conversation, Gina and Bobbi hugged Chrissy in the hallway and headed for civics class while Chrissy headed the other way to study world history, remaining silent and hopeful, trusting in her girls to bring things back from this ledge before she fell over.

Bobbi Li's text this morning stoked that flame of hope to white-hot: "Stay cool and just be your regularly dorky self, girl (lol). If it takes us down to the last second, Chrissy. We got you. Boo Boo and I will never let you down."

When they gathered at lunchtime, Chrissy was the first to speak. "Man, this is our first real crisis, and I don't feel like I'm doing anything to get us through this. I mean it's not only that this whole matter is my fault, but I'm the only 3PG not performing well in this."

They empathized with Chrissy's feeling and knew what response she expected, but they refused to play into that, both opting instead to be very matter-of-fact in pushing right into questions they needed her to answer.

"You get the names of everybody within earshot of that locker room that day." Gina was blunt. "And do you remember the first time Dominique stepped to you? And can you remember exactly what that sleazeball said?"

Bobbi wasn't allowing for any self-pity either. They each tapped information into their phones as Chrissy delivered. And when Chrissy finished, they clasped hands in a circle as Gina spoke softly, "You guys remember when I told you how Grandpa Ricky explained to me what a stick man is and why you can rely on them to find your way out of trouble even when you don't have a clue? And how he explained that a stick man can be a man or woman and how it's who you can depend on to get you through your troubles?"

Gina's eyes were closed as she tightened her grip on their hands, which prompted them to do the same.

"Chrissy, you're clearly the toughest one of us at this table, but your patience and trust will have to be our greater strength right now. You're doing what 3PG is supposed to do, trust in your sisters and believe we'll get you through this. And remember, you don't have just one stick man. Girl, you've got two."

8

BRINGING IT ALL IN

"He dummied up on me last night, Boo Boo."

It was early Saturday morning. Volleyball practice would be in full swing in a few hours, and Bobbi Li was airing frustration about not getting Dominique to come clean about his reasons for pitting Chrissy and Yvonne against one another.

"At first, he tried to blow me off completely, but when I wouldn't relent, that's when the chump hit the mute button on me," said Bobbi Li. "How you doing at being a super sleuth, girl?" She sighed.

"Down to three really serious candidates," said Gina, "and I'm about to get at them right now as a matter of fact. Bobbi, remember, girl, what you're doing will make more sense of this whole thing beyond anything I discover. You just have to figure a way to get that clown to show his hands."

"I know, Gina, but I'm kinda stumped. Got any suggestions?" asked Bobbi Li.

"Just one. What can you hear Nana saying to you if you were with her right now?" Gina shrugged her shoulders and peered into Bobbi Li's eyes with a slight head lean and unwavering seriousness.

Then after what seemed like lengthy, arduous seconds of

thought that twisted her face, Bobbi Li replied in her version of Nana-speak, "You kin catch more flies with sugar than you kin with salt, baby." Then she quickly added with a brisk smile of confidence, "Don't sleep on this Asian girl, Boo Boo. Nana just came through for us again, and I know exactly how I'm going to get this guy to tell us everything we need to know."

The tick-tick of the seconds turning into minutes rushed along and seemed as loud in her brain as the drumbeat of the Energizer Bunny.

"Deep breaths, Bobbi Li. Calm down and think it all through."

Once this crisis has passed and provoked by Gina's revelations, along with Nana having told her at the house, "You wait till them others git through with what they got to tell 'cause what you need to say is all 'bout time, and your timin' gone bring it all together, baby."

She knew there would soon be much for each of them to learn. She had no idea what it all meant but knew she would have to let the girls know about the gifts, the strange new abilities she discovered recently. She initially denied it was real, thinking it to be a machination of her mind, but she was forced to accept its presence and know, instead of going away, it was getting stronger.

After a moment of shock, she could already hear Gina and Chrissy crying with laughter at the irony of it all.

"Hello, Uncle Marlin? It's me, Bobbi Li."

"Mornin', sunshine." The voice on the other end was firm but gentle. "And what would make you think I don't know who I'm talkin' to, young lady?"

"I know, Uncle Marlin. I know. I'm just a little rushed right now, and I really need a big favor from you, if you can do it, please?"

"Anything for my family, baby girl. What do you need?"

Uncle Marlin was none other than Marlin Briscoe, a mild-mannered, unassuming fellow who just happened to have been the first African American in the history of professional football's modern era to be tabbed to start at the quarterback position. On October 6, 1968, he became the starting quarterback for the Denver Broncos of the AFL, before James Shack Harris, Warren Moon, or eventual Super Bowl winners Doug Williams and Russell Wilson. Before any of them were handed the reins of an NFL huddle on Sunday, there was Marlin Oliver (Marlin the Magician) Briscoe.

Built on the same slim and wiry strong frame like an Allen Iverson or Matt Barnes of the NBA, Marlin Briscoe, despite standing five foot eleven and weighing less than 185 pounds for his entire nine-year professional football career, was a stellar performer among the giants of the AFL and the NFL. His rookie season record for passing touchdowns (fourteen) remained a record for the Broncos franchise, being unequaled by the likes of Craig Morton or John Elway, Hall of Famer and two-time Super Bowl winner.

He equaled the Super Bowl wins tally achieved by John Elway by being a two-time winner himself as a member of the legendary, undefeated 1972 Miami Dolphins and again in 1973, as that team would earn back-to-back championships. Converted to wide receiver, he led both those teams in pass receptions even though Hall of Fame wideout Paul Warfield shared the field with him. His four receiving touchdowns in 1972 led an undefeated Dolphins team, along with many of his teammates, right into the record books and the Pro Football Hall of Fame.

One might think such a résumé would establish Marlin Briscoe as a lock for the Pro Football Hall of Fame, but as of 1998, when rabid Oakland Raiders fan and novice football historian, Long Beach City Councilwoman Chun Lau Li met Marlin at a charity function at the Boys and Girls Club, she was livid when told he had not received so much as a nibble at the table of the Hall of Fame.

The very pregnant councilwoman's interest in his status with the Hall of Fame committee was amusing and heartwarming, but her water breaking right there in the community center stole the show, as he and several of the female guests participated in the successful, impromptu birth of a beautiful, kicking, and wailing baby girl who would be named Bobbi Sun Li at Long Beach Memorial Hospital.

To this day, the still-rabid Oakland Raiders fan and now US congresswoman and learned historian of the game of professional football still waged an ongoing campaign with the NFL to correct this slighting of a one-time magnificent champion of the game, still one of her best friends and the godfather to Bobbi Sun Li, Marlin Oliver (Marlin the Magician) Briscoe.

They met in the seclusion of the swimming pool area and sat on the bleachers to begin their second round of conversation, and though he cleared that area to afford them this opportunity, Uncle Marlin was committed to his espial operations, maintaining a vigilant observation of the audio and video feed of their meeting just in case.

"Hey, Dominique. Cool of you to meet with me again, dude."

She extended her hand as a warming gesture, something she hadn't done in their first meeting. For Chrissy's sake, her game must be pure perfection, and she vowed to succeed by any means necessary.

"Sup, china doll?" A mocking, contemptuous tone to his voice quickly dissipated once he took hold of her feathery light, smooth-as-silk hand. "Uh, I know you thinkin' about pumpin' me for info, and I know you still tryin' to help your girl and all, but uh, I still don't know nothin' that's gonna help you. And from what I heard on the streets, ain't it kinda too late anyway?"

"Deep breaths, Bobbi Li. Go get 'im, girl!"

She tightened her grip on his hand while saying, "That doesn't matter as much as what can happen with us right now if you be straight with me, Dominique."

In her seventeen years, not much thought had been given to the feminine wiles that she was now banking on. Having never been in an up-close relationship with a boy before, she really had no opportunity to refine them. And though it wasn't dignified, her sugary allusions would have to be enough to catch this fly, whereas her salty persistence would not.

"Stay on it, girl."

"It might not help Chrissy today, but in the long run, it's going to be a whole lot better for us if we at least know why it went down this way. Then if there is something I can do for you, you got it, dude. But only after you tell me what's up, okay?" The flat-out seriousness of her tone matched the determination in her sparkling, dark brown eyes, which drew him in hypnotically until he could see only what she wanted him to see and hear.

Consequently, being the jerk he was, he could only muster one response to such a provocative proposition, "Damn, china doll, you serious, huh? *The hook was in deep.*"

"Desperately serious, dude." Bobbi was being her best playa-playa.

"I been hearin' ever since I got to Poly about how 3PG are mad tight and there ain't nothin' y'all won't do for each other."

Her feathery light, silken touch and her hypnotic, welcoming gaze had turned his brain into mush and sent the decision of whether or not to cooperate to a part of him just south of his belt line.

"And I get whatever I want right now, right?"

"That's why we're in this place all alone, Dominique."

"You got 'im, girl! Like your mama always said about jerks like this. Promise him anything, but give him a swift kick in the gonads."

Although no one but grandparents or OGs still wore watches with ticking mechanisms in them, for some reason, that sound had gently remained inside her head from the first time her grandfather held his wristwatch up to her ear so she could hear the seconds turning into minutes, ticking away as he explained to her the principles of telling time.

Since the discovery of the gifts, she noticed there were

times the ticking became incessant, allowing her to calculate the timing of an event faster than guesswork or estimations and with an even greater precision when she concentrated as the tick-tick-tick-tick would streamline her focus. And now she was beginning to see ways to manipulate events to her benefit. Tick-tick-tick-tick-tick-tick.

After hurriedly navigating him through tons of irrelevant blah blah blah, she finally extracted the motives for his actions and was thoroughly underwhelmed and disgusted by the selfish, simplistic idiocy of the entire scheme. Her sister and Yvonne were about to lose their entire futures because of some ridiculous conclusion reached by this ignorant knucklehead. She was really pissed. It was time to finish this.

She stood up, took his hand, and led him toward the mats that were in a short stack alongside the bleachers. And his eyes nearly bucked out of his head with delighted anticipation. With anticipation so great that he was one step away from the mats, he took his free hand and grabbed a healthy portion of Bobbi Li's behind, which almost made him blow a fuse from the adrenaline rush.

This also made Uncle Marlin extremely nervous and ready to rush into the pool area, but what unfolded before his eyes within a matter of seconds made him know that someone had made a very wrong choice. Tick-tick-tick-tick-tick-tick.

"Time is at hand now, baby. Don't waste no mo time with trifles. You don't need to seek out all them others. You jest gone 'n' make that call you know will give you the right answer, you hear me?"

Gina heard Nana's voice loud and clear and knew she was right, so acting on Bobbi Li's earlier question, she sat back on the bench in the locker room and closed her eyes. And she was deftly silent.

Ten minutes later, she walked outside, and without hesitation, she dialed Jennifer's number and bluntly asked, "Why did you do this? Why did you put that ring in Chrissy's locker, Jennifer?"

She was merely going through the motions in practice today. And who could blame her for being distracted? Yvonne skipped practice altogether, but she knew that wasn't going to change their scheduled meeting this afternoon. And even though both Gina and Bobbi had encouraged her to just chill and let them work through things, she found that impossible to do.

Call her a chump, a snitch, or whatever. It wasn't that she lacked faith in her girls; nor was fear a factor, as cowardice was a completely abstract notion to the McFarlands. But she had decided earlier this morning to seek help from the one person she knew should be front and center with this imbroglio.

After practice ended and everyone began to disperse, Chrissy headed over to the bleacher area on the football field, the place where destiny was about to make itself known to all.

She kept a slow but steady and confident pace toward the bleachers while focusing on several individuals who were already in that area. Three were standing, and the others were sitting down. But from a distance, it was impossible to tell who they were or whether or not they were boys or girls. The anticipation had quickened her breathing, and her pace was even as she recalled words spoken by her Uncle Sean.

"Anytime them butterflies of doubt started a flutterin' when I stepped inside that ring, darlin', I hurried up to engage my opponent 'cause that's the quickest way to make 'im human-sized, ya know? Stops 'im from bein' a boogeyman, eh? Then I could wallop the crap out of 'im."

Thump-thump-thump-thump. A quickened heartbeat accompanied the huffing of short, anxious puffs of air, like Usain Bolt speeding toward a personal best in the forty-yard dash. She was ready to wallop the crap out of anybody who thought Christiana McFarland would shrink or run from whatever was to come. It was time to make them all human-sized.

Suddenly a beam of recognition penetrated her harried mind as soft sunlight reflected the ensuing calm in her emerald green eyes, now wide open with surprised relief. As each step brought her closer to the assembly in front of the bleachers, she realized the one standing in the middle was the person she had called on this morning and was also the first one to speak in calling out to her.

"If you walk just a little slower, Miss McFarland, we can probably wrap up things sometime before, say, Christmas maybe?" Sarcasm was the favorite tool used by Coach Ameena Johnson when reminding them to hustle in practice.

Chrissy said, "Coming, Coach," and trotted the remainder of the way until she was standing right in front of her.

Dominique was to her right; Jennifer was to her left. And sitting on the first row of the bleachers was Ginger, who was smiling broadly and holding onto Yvonne's right hand while Nana calmly held onto her left. Her 3PG sisters were behind them, giving the thumbs-up sign as they smiled a warm hello to their best bud.

A stick man is a person who is always there for you when you need them but to have two of them is just crazy, stupid good fortune.

9

MISERY DOES LOVE COMPANY

One Month Earlier

Squatting at a secluded corner table at the IHOP on South Street with its façade directly across from Macy's in the Lakewood Mall, Dominique and Jennifer nursed their omelets, short stacks, and the very beginning of their pity party. They would soon learn that feeling sorry for yourself when things are going awry often leads to commissions of desperate acts that can only hurt others and will lack any lasting personal benefits.

"We expect letters of acceptance from the schools Coach Johnson set up for us in another week or two, and I'm so not sure what's going to come in for me. You know I love the ACC, cousin, so I'm hoping for Georgia Tech, North Carolina, or Duke, but I just don't know." Jennifer seemed fraught with anxiety. "It's not like it is for Yvonne and Chrissy Mac, man. They have everybody trying to get them to their campuses. You'd think they were the only 1-A caliber players on our team. It's not like we'd be headed for another state championship if the rest of us weren't ballin' our butts off too." She frowned. Man, I get so tired of those two always glamming it up for the media and all those university reps."

"Well, they are consensus All-American, cuz," Dominique words were heavily laden with derision. "Besides it's the same way with Diamond, ya know? Because he's leading the team in scoring and assists, the focus is always on that guy. Doesn't matter that I'm only percentage points behind him in both categories. And my D is way better. I got more steals than anybody on the squad. If I don't shut down dude playing point for Dominguez last year, we don't win the state."

The most consistent element found in self-pity was being able to gloss over certain aspects of reality and paint a portrait with myopic flair. The fact that Diamond Kincaid, Yvonne Loomis, and Christiana McFarland were also academic All-Americans whose GPAs were several percentage points higher than their own was somehow lost on these two at this moment.

"Don't matter now though," Dominique said, reflecting, "after catching that underage DUI case over the weekend and I ain't even know that fool had weed on 'im either. Don't see much I can do to stop this felony stuff from derailing any scholarship offers I get. Knew I shoulda let Diamond drive his own car to that party Saturday night."

"So what did his pops say after he got y'all outta jail?" she asked.

"He ain't say nothin'. Diamond's folks were in New York at the time, so his pops sent down some high-priced lawyer to get us out."

"Well then, won't the same lawyer rep both of y'all in court?"

"Doubt it. Dude was waitin' for us outside lockup with my car keys in his hand. Don't know how he got them to release it to him, but he handed me my keys and said good night. And then he and Diamond jumped in a silver Range Rover and jetted," he said, sounding unsure.

"So what Diamond say?" She was anxious.

"Said his pops told him to dummy up and chill on the social scene till he can make all the bad stuff disappear. Ain't say nothin' about helpin' me one way or the other. I already peeped this gone be a CYOA thing, cuz, and I'm about to be left out on Front Street." His breathing quickened as he swallowed gloom along with syrupy pancakes.

"You tell your mom yet?" she asked, concerned.

"Nope. Was at the hospital with her yesterday, and all I could think about was how this might blow my chances to play 1-A ball and how disappointed she'll be. Told her I was gonna be a one-and-done with the way her health is 'cause I really need to be helping her out more now. Couldn't bring myself to say anything about the arrest. Figure she'll find out when the court case begins. Just didn't wanna bring no more bad news." He sighed.

"Diamond's folks have so much cheddar. You know he don't have to worry about what happens next while you gotta gut it out with no resources at all. Just ain't right, dude." She fluffed his pity pillow even while stroking his ego, hoping for a reciprocal response.

"If that chump don't look out for me, I'm gonna find a way to bring some pain into that bourgeois life of his, but in the meantime, I thought of a way we can take some of the shine off Yvonne and Chrissy Mac." A sinister grin broke up his face.

"Really?" Thirst was in her voice. "What's up with that?"

"You know Yvonne always had an eye out for your boy, right? Every time I wink at that chick, there's a sparkle in her eyes like she's hungry. She cute, but way too much of an egghead for me though. Asked her a question in biology lab one time, and that chick spit out more technical jargon than the freakin' textbooks. Man, if she and Chrissy Mac could get along, I betcha Yvonne woulda been 3PG a long time ago herself."

"True dat," she concurred. Then a spark of recognition alighted her face. "So you sayin' we find a way to make them bump heads?"

"I already know a way, but it's gonna take you havin' to make a few moves, cuz."

And without hesitation, she smiled. "I'm in, dude."

There was an emotionless, faraway glare in his eyes as he replied, "First, Chrissy Mac and Yvonne. And then you gonna help me holler at that boy Diamond, okay?"

Aiding their subterfuge was the fact that no one at school knew these two knuckleheads were kinfolk.

Two Weeks Ago

"I ain't get even one nibble from the ACC." Jennifer's disappointment twisted her face. "Just a couple of HBCUs, UC Santa Barbara, and San Luis Obispo," Jennifer spoke as if receiving scholarship offers from schools other than the ones she desired were insulting or a reason for despair, which made her salivate at the fiendish update from Dominique, who once again sat across from her in their favorite IHOP in Lakewood.

"Well, the good thing is," he began, "I got your girl's nose wide open already, and her being a virgin made that really easy. Thanks for that tip, cuz. Anyway, after you do your thing, it's all good. If you ain't gone get what you want, man, neither one of those heifers are gonna get what they want either."

And so it began.

Sharing the same booth with them was an unseen and unheard couple whose disdain for these two was immeasurable. As there are two sides to every coin, so too are there to every soul a bright and promising side and a darker, more sinister, and negative side. These uninvited companions were from the latter.

"Brother, these humans are so easily manipulated that it almost seems unfair," one of the observers concluded.

"Unfair or not, my brother," began the other's response, *"we'll thank our ancestors in the long run for that being so, just as long as our manipulation of these weaker ones brings our success."*

10

THE END GAME

Ameena Johnson stood an impressive six feet tall and had cut her teeth in sports at USC playing point forward/shooting guard on the nationally ranked teams that featured the McGee twins, Pamela and Paula; WNBA Hall of Famer Cynthia Cooper; and Cheryl Miller, Hall of Fame scoring machine. Now fifty-one years young, she still maintained a lithe, muscular physique that spoke of her rigorous workout regimen that included swimming three miles four days a week in the Pacific, along with coaching duties that worked in tandem to keep her in excellent shape, kinda hot actually. And though she was very active in community affairs, having to participate in this gathering of individuals connected only by the wrongheaded actions of a couple of young knuckleheads was totally exasperating.

After allowing them both the opportunity to admit their wrongdoings and to vigorously apologize to everyone in attendance, she went on to lay out a plan discussed with Ginger to use her legal expertise to get in front of whatever legal maladies Dominique might have created for himself and form an alliance of sorority and alumni associates with the intent on smoothing his pathway to college, putting everything back on the fast track.

"And Jennifer, my sorority sister who happens to be a tenured liberal arts professor at North Cack-a-lacka, assured me that your application will receive another closer look and is sure something promising can happen for you. All of which points to the fact that, if the two of you had chosen to use intelligence and common sense as your tools to achieve a positive end instead of using the good fortunes of others as fodder for scheming and plotting to create discord, we could have reached this point some time ago."

Although Coach's words blew a breath of freshness over them and whisked away any semblance of the doubt and self-pity that led them to the behavior that prompted this occasion, there was no joy in them. Instead they hung their heads in shame, now realizing how their self-indulgence nearly created a real tragedy for a whole lot of people.

"I am in no way finished with any of you. That means you too, Miss Loomis and Miss McFarland. But we have spent enough time on this foolishness right now, and you three young ladies will report to my office on Monday for further disciplinary measures, as in you will be doing wind sprints until you puke. And, Dominique, you have no idea what Coach Anderson told me is in store for you, dude." Then she added, "I thank you and your mother for your hands-on support, Mrs. Bryant, and I assure you this kind of foolishness will never again be a reason for your presence around here."

She concluded, "Okay, people, seems we're all done here. Loomis and McFarland, make nice before you head out of here. Got that?"

Then she turned and was yards away before either responded. Chrissy and Yvonne moved to the side for a brief one-on-one, concluding with a proper apology to Ginger and Nana for their aberrant behavior.

After all apologies were accepted, Ginger and Nana turned to leave, calling out to Gina and Bobbi Li, "Girls, we'll wait for you all in the car."

Nana told Gina silently, *"Baby, don't make no fuss, but when I held that chile's hand, I could feel it. Somethin' has hold of that girl, and she don't even know it. So this ain't quite over yet, you understand?"*

Gina silently replied. *"Oh, Nana, no!"*

"Enjoy your friends now, baby. We'll talk later," Nana added.

"Yes, ma'am." Then showing no signs of trepidation, Gina turned to Bobbi Li and Chrissy and sighed. "Finally wow, man! How about a group hug, ladies?"

"Not bad for our first real big girl crisis, right?" Bobbi Li assessed while they warmly hugged it out.

"Not bad?" Chrissy was pumped. "You guys were totally awesome!"

"I mean, Gina, how did you know it was Jennifer who had stashed that ring? And you, Bobbi Li, what the heck did you use to get that guy to confess his sins with such conviction?"

"Don't really know how yet." Gina's answer was cloaked in surprise. "But I'm beginning to somehow feel a certain kind of energy when things aren't quite right, like being able to dial into people's impulses. Whatever is happening seems to be refining itself, becoming more definitive." She shrugged. "And to answer your earlier question, Bobbi Li, it does feels like it can be manipulated, like an app for my dreams and my deep thoughts when directed toward the impulses of another person. But I'm with Chrissy on this one, girl. Just how the heck did you finally get that nut to crack?"

Sighing heavily before she spoke, Bobbi Li's answer seemed hushed and embarrassed. "Before I show you guys something, I want you to know that some weird stuff has been happening to me too. I don't know exactly what it is, and now is not the time for discussion. But I can at least answer your questions with this." Pulling her cell phone from her bag, she scrolled to her most recent selfie and said, "This is how I got bright boy to confess. I told him I would post it on Instagram, Facebook, and YouTube unless he did the right thing."

First, Chrissy and Gina looked curiously at the photo and then even more curious at each other. Then they went back at the photo and finally stared at Bobbi Li, totally incredulous.

"Bobbi Li, what the heck is this?" Chrissy started. "I mean, what the heck is going on in this photo?"

"This is way more than just weird, Bobbi Li," Gina chimed in. "Just what the heck are we looking at here? I mean, what are you even doing to this guy?"

The photo showed the diminutive Bobbi Li with her small body wrapped around the six-foot-two frame of Dominique, MMA style, in a way that brought one knee against the joint in his right elbow, another on the back of his neck, and her small hand twisting his wrist in a god-awful fashion that could only have been excruciating, even as she was taking the photo with a free hand.

"Too soon, guys." Bobbi Li flicked her small hand. "Can we just enjoy this small victory today by consuming as much chicken and waffles as Roscoe's can prepare? There is too much stuff to consider about this whole ordeal. Too much we have to talk out and absorb, and I don't want that right now. I don't want to be 3PG. Don't want to be no hero. Just a girl who's got two of the greatest sisters in the world to sit down at a table with and woof down everything placed in front of me, okay?"

As their foreheads touched, each suddenly felt weary, and Gina and Chrissy knew Bobbi Li was right. It was chill time to just be girls.

Then Chrissy added, "I'm going to squat here for a couple seconds just to exhale some, but you guys go on home and get ready. And I'll scoop you up in about an hour and a half. Then we'll go kick the doors in on Roscoe's Chicken 'n' Waffles, all right?"

Gina and Bobbi responded affirmatively as Chrissy extended her clenched fist forward for a fist bump, prompting Gina and Bobbi Li to make it a three-way connection. And they offered in unison words unrehearsed, but absolutely appropriate for this moment. Members of the US Marine Corps proudly proclaim the phrase, "Semper Fidelis," words that mean to be "always faithful" or "once a Marine, always a Marine."

Similarly, from this moment on, the 3PG, with their three-way fist bump would simply proclaim, "Stick man!"

//

OMEGA

Yvonne was somewhat weary when she reached her car parked on the Martin Luther King Boulevard side of the fence surrounding the football field. Her last order of business had been to mean-mug Jennifer with a glare that said, "It's over but not really!" Then she leaned over to whisper choice words into Dominique's ear, and though only the two of them knew what was said, the look on his face was one of distress, spooked even.

Inwardly, she felt silly for allowing herself to be played by Dominique, but since he was the first boy ever to have displayed what seemed like serious amorous intent, she had no way to avoid being duped. She still couldn't understand why she got so pumped to have a blowup with Chrissy Mac and why she had always been plagued by that desire for as long as she could remember. She admired and respected Chrissy in so many ways that this feeling of not being able to like her and always being ready to battle it out with her was baffling. But once again, it didn't happen, and maybe it never would.

The two unseen passengers in the backseat of her red 2004 Chevy Impala could have supplied answers for her, but that was not their mission, as they were the very reason she could never stop reviling Christiana McFarland. Some people called them demons, others said Ifrits or Jinn, and many people dismissed their existence outright, which helped make their mischief-making among us just that much easier. Let us just call these two fiendish entities Ian and Connor.

"We came closer this time, didn't we?" Ian began the discussion.

"Yeah, but close is not why we're here, remember?" Connor reminded him. *"Our job is to make sure this progeny of the Loomis bloodline avenges the wrongs done to our ancestors by the McFarland clan. The curse of the ancients will be lifted once a Loomis has thrashed and incapacitated a McFarland in battle."*

"Aye, but sometimes it seems we'll never find the right one though," Ian reflected. *"Down through the years, we've caused many Loomis and McFarland clashes, but those who represented our bloodline have never proven to be strong enough to upend the McFarlands."*

Connor's grin was crooked. *"Aye, but this one, this little chocolate lassie, would seem to be the right one in the right place at the right time. We'll just have to keep her properly motivated."*

"But what about that old lady, brother? She can feel us, you know? And now she's preparing to teach that young one how to feel us too," Ian voiced real concern.

"The blood of the Loomis clan is stronger than any old lady and her young apprentice," Connor assured him.

"We will succeed this time. Time is on our side. And yes, we will succeed."

By January 1999, the world's undisputed lightweight champion, Sean McFarland, was at the very end of his fighting life. Having won his last four title defenses handily though at age thirty-six, making him a relic in the fight game, he was simply worn down in body, mind, and spirit.

In all his years of fighting, his purses had barely netted him $2 million. Where was his Sugar Ray Leonard, his Tommy Hearns, or his Marvelous Marvin Hagler? His last four title defenses had only been worth $200,000, mere peanuts, he felt. Then just before he was to announce his retirement, a call came from the devil himself.

Don King put an offer on the table, guaranteeing his farewell payday would net him no less than $2.8 million, with pay-per-view concessions adding another quarter million, but only if the fight could happen by May 25, leaving him barely four months to prepare. This was his Sugar Ray Leonard, his Tommy Hearns, and Marvin Hagler rolled into one blanket, as far as he was concerned. So after giving an immediate verbal commitment, he commenced training for the fight and the payday of his life.

His opponent was the present European champion, a twenty-six-year-old guy named Bryce Maynard who was from the bowels of the Enfield area of London, and though Maynard sported an impressive twenty-four and zip record with twenty-two wins by knockout, Sean could have cared less. The guy could have been the undefeated half-brother of Godzilla, but for nearly $3 million, Sean still would have fought him, home or away.

That fight went on to become an instant classic and was also voted Fight of the Year for 1999 by all boxing standards. It was one of the most brutal fights ever witnessed in the modern era, and since Sean wound up taking a vicious pounding that night, if he hadn't already committed to retirement, it was of no matter. His body was devastated during the bout.

He had never even heard of Bryce Maynard, who seemed to just magically appear on the horizon. Nor had he ever fought anyone who fought as savagely and hit so thunderously, but money aside, losing his final bout was not an option. So after being downed once in each of the first three rounds, Sean became the ultimate ring manager by staying at a distance with a Larry Holmes-style, piston-like jab and by employing every ring ruse gleaned from hours of studying videos of the GOAT, Muhammad Ali, ever since his first AAU bouts as a teen. He willfully and artfully outpointed the dangerous slugger over twelve rounds to win eight rounds to three with one even round. Never again would a pair of boxing gloves be laced up on the hands of Sean McFarland.

During that fight, there seemed to be two curiously empty ringside seats, but they were actually being held down by a couple of unseen interlopers who originally discovered Bryce Maynard in England and were betting their very existence on this guy, who fought under the family name of his adoptive father, Kyle Maynard. His birth father was a highly successful, white-collar, career criminal whom current Interpol records identified as Chauncey Loomis.

12

MUSING

As Chrissy sat alone on the bleachers, winding down and allowing her thoughts to resettle, she beamed at how valiantly her sisters fought to protect her, even from herself. She flushed with embarrassment at how ego and pride had overridden her intelligence, causing her to succumb to emotionalism and spiral out of control, making her very willing to bite off more than she could chew and foolishly offer herself up to the evils of the world as an equal part of a two-for-one meal for losers. But she was no loser, and neither were her girls. They were 3PG, and always striving toward their very best was how they rolled. Her sisters had come up big for her in every way, and she felt blessed to have real love in her heart for two crazy girls who really loved her.

Even now, as they seemed to be strangely and miraculously morphing into versions of themselves neither of them could possibly have imagined—versions that would require a mastermind alliance of sorts to ascertain what it all meant.

Then suddenly, a scolding voice zipped into her head loud and strong. *"Red, the next time I say for you to tell them other two what needs tellin', that means you tell it all to 'em, not jest the parts you want to tell. I meant all of it. You hear me, young lady?"*

"Nana?!"

"Are you sure, Mama?" Ginger was sitting cross-legged between Nana's legs while her hair was being parted with her scalp gently scratched and massaged.

And finally a light spray of sesame oil would be applied to soothe the nerves. This was the same way it had been done for her in all her lifetime. It was hair-doin' time, and while the girls were having their chill-out dinner, Ginger and Nana were sharing a tender moment.

"Baby, I'm as sure of this as I am of all the love we both have for our chile." Nana's voice was calm and confident. "She done accepted the gift she been given, and she's so smart that she already kin see lots of ways to help other people by using it."

"But how can you be sure it won't hurt her the way it hurt me?"

"If you remember back when you was little 'n' had your first dreams, you know they never was that clear. And they scared you so bad that it give you real bad headaches. Boo Boo don't get no headaches. Ain't never been scared by nothing in them dreams. And the details in 'em are real for her, honey, right down to the colors 'n' smells of everythang in 'em. And even the biggest old fool in this world knows dreams don't come in colors, so it can only because the Lord say so. She startin' to embrace it, baby, even told me what she done named it."

"What she named it?" Ginger was in full surprise mode.

"She calls it her dream app, whatever that means to these young folk." Holding Ginger's head back and looking into her eyes, she continued. "You gone have to tell her 'bout your dreams 'n' that you understand what she got 'n' that everythang gone be all right for us. She needs to hear that from you, baby."

"I know, Mama." A smile of calm was on her face. "I just worry about her and want my baby to be safe. Don't want her hurt."

"She 'bout safe as she can ever be, baby." Nana kissed Ginger's forehead gently and continued. "She got the love of her family and them two crazy girlfriends of hers, but mostly it's 'cause of what we always say in church 'n' what we supposed to be livin' our life 'bout, right?"

Simultaneously and harmoniously, Nana and Ginger chimed, "If the Lord brings you to it, He'll bring you through it."

EPILOGUE

"It's our night tonight, Boo Boo."

Ginger sat in Nana's favorite chair, surrounded by all the hair-doin' products with a fluffy pillow between her legs, which Gina always sat on when getting her hair treated. The warmest smile invited her to that familiar spot.

"This will be Nana's night off, okay? It's my turn to do that fine bush of hair on your head while we have ourselves a big girl talk about your dream app."

Today would not be that day, of course, as any more revelations concerning the changes they were experiencing would have just been too weird. It would have pushed them all into overload. The chicken and waffles, along with the laughter and joke-filled camaraderie, was exactly what was needed to loosen up and make them feel normal again.

But in the solitude of her bedroom as she sat astride the bed, looking over a sea of offers from prospective universities, Chrissy knew Nana's admonition was serious. She also knew it was the right thing to do. Nana already knowing about Chrissy's personal changes without one spoken word about them just seemed to be par for the course because that was who she was, and knowing was what she did.

The girls would assemble at the McFarland household after church tomorrow, and she would make her presentations about recently discovered gifts, abilities she now felt ashamed at having had the slightest impulse of using in that ridiculous blowup with Yvonne. Contemplating the impossible probability of the full measure of changes happening to her sisters covered Chrissy in melancholy, creating a nervousness as to how they would manage those full disclosures and how those revelations would certainly open new doors and alter everything in their lives.

Sitting across from her grandfather at the antique teak card table, ready to begin their second chess match, Bobbi Li wondered what his response would be when she opened up to him.

"Granddad, I have something really strange to share with you."

"I have already witnessed your calculated moves on this chessboard, little one. They seem so much more precise." Showing no surprise, the old man, who'd once held a wristwatch to the ear of a small child to teach her how to tell time, smiled broadly. "I would guess we are now going to speak about how you have learned to set your pace to the natural cadence of time."

Printed in the United States
By Bookmasters